W9-AQX-953

Property of
Louisville Public Library

E
GAU
c.1

ZACHARY in
The Present

by Bertrand Gauthier
illustrations by Daniel Sylvestre

For a free color catalog describing Gareth Stevens's list of high-quality books, call 1-800-341-3569 (USA) or 1-800-461-9120 (Canada).

Library of Congress Cataloging-in-Publication Data

Gauthier, Bertrand, 1945-
    [Zunik dans la surprise. English]
    Zachary in The present / text by Bertrand Gauthier ; illustrated by Daniel Sylvestre.
       p. cm. — (Just me and my dad)
    "Original edition published in 1987 by Les éditions la courte échelle inc., Montréal, under the title: Zunik dans la surprise" — T.p. verso.
    Summary: Zachary's excitement grows as he searches for the present his father has hidden.
    ISBN 0-8368-1010-4
    [1. Fathers and sons—Fiction. 2. Gifts—Fiction.] I. Sylvestre, Daniel, ill. II. Title: The present. III. Series.
PZ7.G2343Zadf 1993
[E]—dc20
                                       93-7719

This edition first published in 1993 by
Gareth Stevens Publishing
1555 North RiverCenter Drive, Suite 201
Milwaukee, Wisconsin 53212, USA

This edition first published in 1993 by Gareth Stevens, Inc. Original edition published in 1987 by Les éditions la courte échelle inc., Montréal, under the title *Zunik dans la surprise*. Text © 1987 by Bertrand Gauthier. Illustrations © 1987 by Daniel Sylvestre.

All rights to this edition reserved to Gareth Stevens, Inc. No part of this book may be reproduced, stored in a retrieval system, or transmitted in any form or by any means, electronic, mechanical, photocopying, recording, or otherwise, without the prior written permission of the publisher except for the inclusion of brief quotations in an acknowledged review.

Series editor: Patricia Lantier-Sampon
Series designer: Karen Knutson

Printed in the United States of America
1 2 3 4 5 6 7 8 9 97 96 95 94 93

At this time, Gareth Stevens, Inc., does not use 100 percent recycled paper, although the paper used in our books does contain about 30 percent recycled fiber. This decision was made after a careful study of current recycling procedures revealed their dubious environmental benefits. We will continue to explore recycling options.

Gareth Stevens Publishing
MILWAUKEE

Property of
Louisville Public Library

What a beautiful day! Everybody is outside in the park.

I always have fun in the park. I like the sandbox, the teeter-totter, and the swings.

Today, I wish my father had not come to get me so soon. You see, Yoyo Mikado and I are building a city in outer space.

I bet I know what it is! My father has finally bought me the electronic wawabongbong I've always wanted.

My father says I get the hiccups when I get too excited. But it's hard not to get excited when you're going to have an electronic wawabongbong.

My father always hides presents in his room.

You're cold, Zach. You've never seen a present like this one. Go look in your room.

I've looked everywhere. Maybe it's just a trick. My father plays tricks on me sometimes.

Then I see my present. It's right on my pillow.

I open it as fast as I can. But it's not an
electronic wawabongbong.

My father tells me to sit down, close my eyes, and open my ears.

What a surprise! Mama is talking inside the tape recorder.

 18

Mama lives in New York now. And she is inviting me to come stay with her for a week.

At dinner, my father tells me all about New York and the skyscrapers they have there.

After we eat, I draw a picture of
Mama's house. I haven't finished my
drawing, but it is time to go to bed.

...and there are wawabongbongs flying through the air, and they are as high as the airplanes and the clouds, and they can see over the horizon.

When I can't fall asleep, my father always tells me a long, long story.

I love my mother when she sends me a
present like that.